AN MMF FORBIDDEN ROMANCE

CLUELESS

C. S. SILVERNE

Copy and Line Editing by Sadie, Dot The i Edit

Cover Artwork: Valerie

Interior Formatting: Disturbed Valkyrie Designs (@disturbedvalkyriedesigns)

PLAYLIST

Needed Me — Rihanna
PILLOWTALK — ZAYN
if u think i'm pretty — Artemas
older — Isabel LaRosa
Cool for the Summer — Demi Lovato
Squeeze — Ghostemane
Bad Things — mgk, Camila Cabello
Lavender Haze — Taylor Swift
love me — Ex Habit
Ghost Inside The Shell — Catch Your Breath
Greedy — Tate McRae
Angel With A Shotgun — The Cab
HOT DEMON B!TCHES NEAR U !!! — CORPSE,
Night Lovell
Tears Don't Fall — Bullet For My Valentine

Shameless — Camila Cabello

Whistle — Flo Rida

Dark Horse — Katy Perry, Juicy J

exes — Tate McRae

Cupid's Chokehold — Gym Class Heroes

Alkaline — Sleep Token

Timber — Pitbull, Kesha

LOVE. FEAT ZACARI. — Kendrick Lamar, Zacari

Promiscuous — Nelly Furtado, Timbaland

Midnight Rain — Taylor Swift

Listen to the full playlist here <3

CONTENT

Clueless contains content that may be sensitive to some. *Please protect yourself and your mental health.*

Age gap (19 years), alcohol use/consumption, anxiety, depression, injuries from the military (side character), mention of military accident (not on page), mention of parental abuse (past, not on page), mention of parental death (not on page), mentions of previous sexual partners, mentions of tubal ligation, military main characters, miscommunication, pregnancy (side character), PTSD (military & childhood trauma based), self-slut-shaming, strained sibling relationships,

& taboo relationships prior to meeting FMC (step-dad & step-son).

Sexual content includes anal sex, BDSM power dynamics, blowjobs & deep-throating, biting, breeding kink (no pregnancy), choking/breath play, cunnilingus, daddy + little girl/little boy play (no age play), degradation kink, double vaginal penetration, edging as punishment, explicit sex scenes, frotting, light exhibitionism (backyard/patio), light humiliation, masturbation, praise kink, sex at a glory hole, sexual activity while drunk/after drinking, sexual sharing (step-dad/step-son & girlfriend), somnophilia (non-con/CNC), spitting in mouths and on genitalia, squirting, threesomes, and use of sex toys.

Disclaimer:

Clueless is an extremely forbidden short novella with *little-to-no plot* set in the Reckless Hearts world. If you are looking for a book with substance, you won't find that here. However, if you are looking for a short story with dirty talking military men who like to share...

enjoy!

RESOURCES

Clueless briefly touches on themes of parental abuse, depression, and depression stemming from PTSD. While this story is fictional and marketed as erotica, I know these experiences are very real—and that so many people live through them every single day. I, myself, have struggled before, and I know that feeling lost and lonely can be absolutely debilitating.

With the help of others, I've included links below to charities, organizations, and other resources that might offer support.

Regardless of what you've experienced and who has told you otherwise, you're a total badass, and you're not alone.

XO,

C. S. Silverne

988 Lifeline (National Suicide Prevention Lifeline) — Call or text 988 for immediate mental health support

National Alliance on Mental Illness (NAMI) HelpLine
National Association of Adult Survivors of Child Abuse

To those who have felt lonely, even when surrounded by everyone.

To those who have felt clueless and lost, yet continue to stumble through life anyway.

...and to those who have met someone's stepdad and immediately thought, "Holy shit... do you need a new mom?"

ONE

A SIGH LEAVES my lips for the umpteenth time that hour as I scroll through my plethora of text messages and social media notifications, nursing the fruity cocktail in front of me. As much as I have loved attending my brother's wedding this evening, it was yet another reminder that I can never shake this...empty feeling inside of me—a feeling only highlighted when I'm near my siblings, let alone their partners.

At least Daddy dearest died before the wedding. I haven't had to deal with any of his narcissistic, abusive words. I'm sure he is rolling in his grave over Aiden being genuinely, truly happy.

I shake my head, trying to clear my thoughts. Tonight was supposed to be a good night. It *was* a good night. Rory looked absolutely beautiful in her wedding gown, and I shed more than a few tears over the fact that I *finally* get to call someone my sister. I've already called Casey my brother for years now. The night was magical, and I couldn't be happier for my siblings or their children.

They're *happy*.

I just wish I knew how to be happy, too.

The sound of a chair sliding out beside me forces me out of my thoughts entirely, and I look up into the eyes of a man that has to be in his forties. He looks down at the chair before looking back at me. "Is this seat taken?"

I shake my head. "Go ahead."

Though, I don't *not* notice how the bar is pretty much empty, and he's choosing to sit directly next to me. A part of my mind is screaming *stranger danger*, but the other part of my mind is focusing on just how much my feet hurt from these heels, and I don't want to run away unless I absolutely have to.

He speaks again. "I don't think I've seen you here before. What brings you to this shithole?"

I look around the bar, questioning where the hell this "*shithole*" is that he's referring to. This is the nicest bar I've been to in a long time. The real question is— why the fuck is it so empty if it's this nice? Turning back to him, I raised a pointed brow. "Dare I say, we have different definitions of shitholes."

He barks out a laugh, and somehow, it fills me with a sense of butterflies. "Really now?"

I smile as I pull my drink closer to me, pleased with myself. As much as I wish I had the whole "man-hating" gene in me, I do indeed take far more pride in making a man who looks like a pit bull laugh. "Yeah. This place is very nice. I keep wondering why it's empty."

He smirks down at me. "It's about to close."

My mouth goes into the shape of an *O*. "Should I leave?"

The man shakes his head before signaling to the bartender. "Nah. You still have some time. This rounds on me, okay?"

I look down into the bottom of my drink, confused, until I realize that it's definitely empty.

When the fuck did I drink all of it?

Should I even have another one, if that's the case?

With my mood tonight, I refuse to even let myself psychoanalyze that. "Sure. Okay. But the bartender hands it to me first."

He looks back at me and raises an eyebrow questioningly.

I shrug. "What? I don't know you. You could roofie me."

The bartender whose name tag says *Steven* laughs, though he follows it with a cough, trying to hide it. I bite back my own tipsy laugh. The man beside me only shakes his head. "Tequila sunrise for me tonight, please. And the lady will have…"

I stare at my drink, contemplating. "Actually, I'll have the same. Gold tequila though, please."

Steven knocks on the counter in response to both of us before he gets to work. I play around with the straw in my drink, musing as to how to even start a conversation with this man that happens to look like a Greek God, but he beats me to it. "So, you never answered my question. What brings you here? You've been here awhile."

I raise an eyebrow. "Been watching me?"

"Can't help but notice and admire beauty when it comes in."

That gets a snort out of me. "Cheesy. Just looking to escape, though. I just moved here from Nashville, and my brother got married tonight."

He pauses. "So, you came to a bar? Is there no alcohol at your brother's wedding?"

"Oh, there is. But you can only be around so many lovey-dovey people before you want to gouge your eyes out."

The man whistles. "Harsh."

"But truthful. I love both of my brother's partners. Don't get me wrong. I've just been in an odd place lately, I guess."

Steven comes back then, setting the drinks on the bar top. His voice is deep and masculine as he speaks, pausing our conversation. "Order up, Boss. Should I head out?"

I swivel my head to the man next to me, shocked. He nods to Steven. "Yeah, man. Be safe. Lock up behind you, if you don't mind."

Steven nods before leaving the bar area entirely, but my gaze is still on the man next to me. He chuckles. "Yes, ma'am?"

"You own this place?"

"I do."

"Wha...but..." I pause. "Huh?"

He laughs again before nodding to the drink in front of me. "You sure you can handle drinking another one?"

My face immediately drops as I grab it. *Prick.* "I'm fine, thank you. You're just an enigma; I don't know how to read you."

As I go to take a sip of my drink, I'm frozen solid when he leans down and whispers in my ear. His beard tickles my exposed skin, forcing goose bumps across my flesh instantly. "Such a fancy word for such a little girl."

Fuck. Me.

I know without a doubt in my mind that any other girl would have thrown her drink in his face and stormed out. And yet…I think I need to change my panties.

I clear my throat, trying to regain my composure. It doesn't work, but I happen to be a very good bull-shitter. "What's your name?"

"Sean."

"Alright, Sean," I say. "Why are you really letting me stay in your bar?"

"Do you want the truthful answer or the bullshit answer?"

I pin him with a stare as my answer to that question.

He smirks as he sips his drink. "You looked lonely and miserable, and misery loves company."

I blink. *Ouch.*

That's what I get for wanting the truth.

He speaks again. "Like I said, little girl—misery loves company. I had a rough day, too. Don't read into it more than you should."

Like a puppet on strings, my overthinking zips away in an instant.

Fucking daddy issues.

I hate it here.

I take a big sip of my drink as I ask my next question. "Why was your day miserable?" Sean looks like he's weighing his options, and I say my next thought before he can bullshit me. "Let's make a deal. We say the complete and utter truth whenever we're talking to each other."

That makes him pause. "What happens if we don't?"

I giggle. "We punish the other."

His eyebrows rise, and it's only then I notice the gray hairs coming in at his temples. The sight makes me swallow roughly, and I turn back toward my drink. *I am definitely starting to feel the alcohol.*

He shrugs. "Deal. Day was miserable because my girl dumped me and my stepson. Well, our girl."

My body goes still for a second. "Come again?"

It's his turn to take big swallows of his drink. "To which part?"

"You *and* your stepson?"

His eyes are hooded as he looks down at me. "Yes."

"How does that work?"

Sean shrugs again. "I share with him. He shares with me. She didn't want to do it anymore. I'll never force a woman into anything she doesn't want to do, but I also will never risk my relationship with my stepson. So, we both let her go."

"Huh..." I say, trying to wrap my head around what I've just been told. I'm in absolutely no place to judge, but that has got to be a new one.

He clears his throat. "You said we tell the truth."

I swivel my head to him. "What? I'm not judging you or anything."

He squints. "You're not?"

I laugh. "Are you kidding? I just told you that my brother was polyamorous, and I've had my share of threesomes when I was in college. I have fully learned that you like what you like. I'm just...did you like, raise him, too, or...?"

His eyes widen. "Oh my God, no! No. His mom and I got married *and* divorced when he was nineteen, but she's...a pretty sore excuse for a mother, so he and I stayed in touch. It was right when he joined the military. So, he's technically not even my stepson anymore. I guess we're just friends now, technically."

I hold my hands up in surrender. "Can't blame a girl for thinking it. I didn't know how taboo we were talking." Silence envelopes us for setting before I ask another question. "Do you and him...?"

The blush on his face is the only answer I need, but he answers anyway. "We have. Not often. More so testing boundaries and sexualities. But we have." He quickly steers the conversation away. "Threesomes in college, eh? How old are you?"

"I'm twenty-six. You?"

"Forty-five."

"Experienced," I muse before slapping a hand over my mouth. "I'm so sorry. It just slipped."

Sean bellows a laugh that shakes his entire body as he responds. "Don't worry about it. I thought the same about you."

I blush. "You could say that."

"What's the wildest thing you've done?" he questions, standing up and going behind the bar to make another drink. I didn't even realize he drank all of his. I pout as I look at my drink, still half-full.

"Just like that? Down to the dirty?"

"I'm a curious man."

I laugh, shrugging. The likelihood of me seeing this man after tonight is little-to-none. Virginia Beach is a big city. What do I have to lose? "My college graduation party, my boyfriend at the time and his best friends shared me."

Sean pauses. "And how many friends was that?"

I bite my lip. "A few."

He raises a brow. "Airtight?"

My thighs clench as I think back to that night. I leave out the part about it being my birthday gift—and that Kyle was also receiving from said friends. The definition of a wild night. "Yup."

My eyes jump up at the sound of Sean dropping a cocktail jigger. He curses and immediately goes to wiping up the mess.

I pause. "Should I take that as a compliment or an insult?"

His eyes are heavy when they hit me again. "Compliment. Fighting a boner here, little girl."

Yup. Definitely need to change my panties.

My breath comes out heavy. "Keep calling me that and we're going to have problems."

I swear I hear what sounds like a growl come out of him, but he merely shakes his head. "You have another question?"

I smirk. "How did you know I did?"

"Because your response was also a question."

My lips twitch. "Fair point. Yes, I do. When did you and your stepson start sharing women? How did that even happen? It didn't start with his mom or anything, did it?"

"Ew, gross." His nose wrinkles. "I hardly even wanted to have sex with just her."

I raise an eyebrow, waiting.

He shrugs. "Around when I left the military, five or so years ago, he and I went to a bar and it just... happened. We were an exclusive throuple for a year or so. It was fantastic." He stands up straighter, confident in his words. "No one ever having to worry about being lonely. All needs, physical and emotional, taken care of. It just worked. And I've been alive long enough —seen enough—to know that when something is right, you don't test it."

"That sounds nice. Not being lonely or longing."

The words slip out before I can shush them. I close my eyes briefly, knowing I'm likely making a fool of myself.

"It is."

Opening my eyes again, I lock eyes with him, and he speaks again. "Are you lonely, little girl?"

I don't even hesitate. "I've always been lonely."

"Even with siblings?"

My shoulders lift in a shrug. "Brothers can't erase an abusive dad who calls you names and forces you into isolation. Even if they tried to protect me."

The air is silent for a second. Heavy. A part of me wants to apologize, but I've also worked very hard with my therapist in the last few years to accept the fact that my past is just that—my past. And if we're being truthful with each other, then it's just a part of me.

His voice is heavy when he responds. "I'm sorry to hear that."

I move the topic back to sexy-land. It was far more enjoyable—even if the majority of the population would undoubtedly call me and the man before me every crude word in the book. "So, you're experienced. But what's something you haven't done in a long time, that you want to do soon?"

His gaze penetrates my soul as he responds. "I haven't fucked a woman one-on-one in a long time."

Instantly, my mouth goes dry. I almost have to force my next words out. "Do you want to?"

"Very much so."

Oh...my God.

Before I can respond, he asks his next question. "What's something you want to do that you've never done? Coming from an experienced girl."

I sit on it for a second, musing. My response comes out dry and filled with humor, knowing it's something that will likely never happen. "Never done the whole glory-hole thing. Sounds hot, though. I've watched a lot of porn with it."

Sean doesn't laugh with me, though.

He smirks.

TWO

THE WOMAN before me has me utterly captivated, all the way from her blonde hair and brown highlights down to her strap-on heels. She's enchanted me from the moment she stepped in my bar, and a part of me—while disappointed, sure—is grateful that Allison cut ties with Noah and I this morning.

Via text.

The thought makes my eyes roll. It's the last time I let Noah pick the girl, that's for sure. From that moment on, I told him that anyone we shared would have to have their frontal lobe fully developed.

But the woman before me...well, that's not a concern.

And she knows what she wants, too.

I clear my throat. The alcohol is starting to relax

me, and I want nothing more than to make the woman in front of me delirious from alcohol *and* my cock. "What if I told you that I could make that happen for you?"

Her pink-stained lips pop open. "What?"

I smirk down at her and grip the bar top to keep from putting my hands on her so soon. "I know a place. Never done it either, actually. But I know where I can make that fantasy come true for you."

She stares at me for what feels like an eternity until she says, "Okay."

"Okay?"

"Are you going to hurt me?" she asks.

"Absolutely not," I reassure her. Granted, even someone who was going to hurt her would respond that exact same way, but I'm not going to tell her that. I may have just met this woman tonight, but I already know she thinks more than she breathes. "You're safe with me, little girl."

She melts into the chair at my words. Deep satisfaction fills me as I walk around the bar and hold out my hand. If she takes it, then I'm going to ruin her in the best of ways. If she doesn't, then there will be an Uber on the way within minutes. I ask the question pressing at my brain, though. "What's your name, sweetheart?"

And when electricity shoots up my hand as she takes it, I know I'm completely and utterly fucked.

"Lauren."

LAUREN WAS QUIET THE ENTIRE DRIVE HERE, and a part of me is nervous that I scared her off when I started feeding her water and carbs.

Okay, a lot of me is nervous.

But for fuck's sake, I'm not actually going to take advantage of a drunk girl half my age. I may be into some weird, kinky shit—but I do draw the line at rape. It's been hours since I offered to make her fantasy come true, but she needed time to sober up entirely.

I swallow nervously as I park my truck in the parking lot of the Motel 6. Because who else would have a sketchy-as-fuck glory hole? I crane my neck to look at her, pausing when I find her eyes already searching my face. "Do you want this, Lauren? Because I can and will take you home."

She bites her lip, and I swear my dick twitches in my jeans. "I think so."

I cock an eyebrow. "I'm gonna need you to *know so*, sweetheart."

She bites back a smile. "Are you always so firm?"

Deciding to take a risk from hell, I lean over the center console, unbuckle her seatbelt, and lift her out of the passenger seat entirely. She squeals and grabs ahold of my shoulders as I position her to straddle my lap. I smirk up at her, moving my hands to her waist. "I was a Master Sergeant in the Marine Corps, and I'm a grown man who knows what he wants. Safe to say that *firm* is my default, yeah."

Her eyes stay locked on my lips. "I want this. But..."

"But?" I prompt.

"But you haven't even kissed me yet. I'm afraid I can't suck your cock like we both need until that's rectified, *Sergeant*."

I groan.

I've been wanting to do this for fucking hours, but I also wanted to make sure the glassy look in her eyes was gone first. Now, with her in my lap, directly in front of my face, I can see it's fully gone, and my restraint is being pulled like a tightrope. "Then kiss me, little girl."

She doesn't hesitate.

In milliseconds, her mouth is molded to mine, her hands gripping my face tightly. And the kiss is anything but sweet. It's hot, feverish, uncontrolled. Her tongue finds mine immediately, swiping at it. The taste of cherries invade my senses, and I want nothing more than to taste every single inch of her.

Lauren pulls back, eyes heavy and hooded. Her lips

are swollen, lower face the slightest bit agitated from the scruff of my beard. "Sean?"

My voice is hoarse. "Yeah?"

"I want this."

Thank fuck.

I grab the back of her head and slam my mouth to hers this time, desperately needing to devour her. I genuinely can't get enough of her, and I already know I'm going to be sad when this night officially comes to an end.

As if she can read my thoughts, she pulls away. "What happens after this?"

I stare at her. "I take you home."

"Will I see you again?"

Raising a hand, I wipe at my beard. "I don't know."

The answer makes her pause, and for a second, I wonder if I've completely fucked everything up. But I promised her that I would be honest, and while a one-night stand and kinky shenanigans sound fantastic, I don't know if I'm ready for anything more so soon.

Let alone Noah.

Just as I go to lift her off me, accepting what is, she shocks me by pressing against me and forcing a hiss out of my mouth. "Whatever. Make my fantasy come true. We have tonight."

THREE

1.5 YEARS LATER

"YOU LOOK ABSOLUTELY STUNNING," I say to Lauren as she climbs into my truck. I just got off work and I almost don't even feel worthy enough to be in her presence, all dirty and still in my camos. But it was a shitty day, and I wanted nothing more than to be around the one human who knows how to make me smile at all times.

The one human who I'm falling in love with.

The thought and feeling sits heavy in my chest as I stare at the girl next to me. We've only been dating for five months, but I swear, she feels like the one.

God, I hope Sean likes her.

More than that, I hope she doesn't freak the fuck

out tonight. Most anyone would…but there's a part of me hoping for a miracle. The imaginary conversation has played on loop in my head for weeks.

"Hey, Lauren. This is my once stepdad, Sean. We both want to fuck you now. And keep you forever. We may also fuck from time to time, too. Is that cool?"

Shouldn't be a disaster at all. *Pffft.*

Yeah, right. Anxiety surrounds me like a barricade at the dozens of possibilities for the night ahead. She could shrug it off, and we could break the sharing cycle entirely. She could freak the fuck out and run away. She could be willing to try it.

And yeah, it's not required. Not at all.

Sean has been hung up on some random one-night stand he had over a year ago. I don't even know if he wants to start anything new. But I do know that the both of us agreed—years ago—that it made us happy, even if it was fucked up.

So, why not?

The previous girls were different, though. They wanted sex first and foremost, and it was only the relationship piece that scared them off. It's why every single one of them has either left, cheated, or started to favor one of us, rather than both of us.

But Lauren just feels…different.

And fuck, am I scared to death of fucking up.

Her voice snaps me out of my overthinking cycle.

She smooths down an invisible wrinkle in her white crop top nervously before patting her right leg that just so happens to be covered in a full tattoo sleeve. "Yeah? Not too slutty or anything, right?"

I scoff, meeting her brown eyes. "It's summer. And we live on the beach. You could be parading around in a thong and not worry about that."

Lauren meets me with a droll stare. "I'm about to meet an important figure in your life for the first time! I'm not trying to look like a whore, Noah."

I shake my head. She's curled her hair, too. The pure-white low-lights peek through her midnight hair in stark contrast. And it's then that I realize she *really* put a lot of effort into her appearance.

She hates curling her hair.

I reach over and tug a lock of it, forcing her to me. She gasps, and I take it as my opportunity to kiss her, slowly and affectionately. When I pull away, a blush mars her skin, and I smile softly. "You look beautiful. Now, let's go to my place so I can get cleaned up, and then we can go wish this grumpy old man a happy birthday."

Steam wafts out of the bathroom as I wrap a towel around my waist, and grab my phone off the bathroom counter.

ME

Hey. On the way. Bringing a girl, FYI.

SEAN

A girl?

ME

…yeah. Sorry.

SEAN

blank stare gif

Jesus, kid. Give a man some warning.

ME

I did. You have ten minutes

SEAN

Brat.

What's her name?

ME

Lauren.

I think you'll like her.

There's a pause in the text thread, and I walk in the living room, finding Lauren petting a very tired Rocco as she scrolls on her phone.

I pout at my girlfriend and dog. "I want to be petted."

Lauren turns to me and raises an eyebrow. "I'm gonna have to pass on the whole animal-play thing."

My mouth drops. "Oh, c'mon. But I have the best puppy-dog eyes ever."

She merely rolls her brown ones before turning back to her phone. "Go put some clothes on, nerd. Your stepdad is gonna disown you and hate me before we're even there."

Doubtful.

I stare at her. "You know he's not still my stepdad, right? I'm technically already disowned."

She glares at me over her phone.

Chuckling, I do as I'm told and turn towards my bedroom, right as my phone buzzes again.

SEAN

Lauren? She doesn't have blonde hair, does she?

With brown in it?

I squint down at my phone, confused.

ME

No??? Black and white.

SEAN

Oh. Ok

ME

Do I wanna know?

SEAN

No. See you both soon.

26

Shrugging, I toss my phone onto the bed and start getting dressed. Cryptic answers are nothing new from the man, and we are definitely going to be late. I'll press him about it in person later.

Instead, my mind wanders to the outcome of tonight, yet again.

Here goes fucking nothing.

FOUR

LAUREN

"OKAY," I start, right as the GPS says we're three minutes from Noah's stepdad's house. "Give me the *Dad* pep talk. You talk about him fondly, and I don't want to fuck this up."

Noah turns to me, smirking. His tattooed arm takes over the wheel while his right hand comes up to pat my leg. "Nervous about fucking up, eh? This feels serious. And, babe, he's *not* my dad."

I shove his shoulder. "Would you stop cracking jokes? I'm scared! And it's dad-esk, okay? I really like you, but I quite literally do not have a good example of a dad, and therefore, I need to impress one of yours since I never impressed mine."

"Okay, okay. What to say..."

I motion for him to keep talking with my hands,

forcing a laugh out of him. "He served in the Marines. He was pretty high rank, so he can be scary sometimes, but he's truly all bark and no bite to the people he likes."

My stomach drops. "Oh, good. So, if he bites, then I'm out. Yippee."

He shakes his head. "Shhhhh. You'll be fine."

I almost whimper as I stare out at the passing trees. "Keep going."

"Uhm, ever since he got out of the military, he's been dabbling in multiple forms of entrepreneurship. And I mean, *multiple*. Dude owns way too many businesses now. So, you can always talk shop with him. See what his favorite one of the week is."

I nod, absorbing the information as I turn back to him. "Okay. Does he have a girlfriend or wife? Someone to break the ice with if Mr. Scary turns Mr. Terrifying?"

Noah coughs once, and then twice—almost like he's choking on his own spit. His grip turns firm on the steering wheel. "N-no. Nothing like that."

I squint at him but decide not to press it. I have enough anxiety over this whole thing already, and knowing Noah mentioned once that his mother pretty much walked out on him entirely when he turned into an adult, I'm sure that is a memory path that we want to fully avoid today.

As we pull into the driveway of a house with way too many cars parked around us, my mouth drops. "*This* is his house?"

Noah cuts the engine and leaps out of the truck. He rounds the vehicle and opens my door, offering me his hand.

Just like that, butterflies swarm me.

He chuckles at my expression and presses a kiss to the top of my forehead. "You're cute. This is his house, indeed. My house, sometimes, when I decide to stay here. Depends on the circumstances."

I move my gaze back from him to the house. "Entrepreneurship, huh? I really need to quit my marketing job and start my own agency, if this is the affect."

He forces a smile then and tugs me to him before I can walk up the driveway. "Lauren...whatever happens tonight, just know I really like you. Okay?"

I blink. "I'm not about to get sacrificed, am I?"

He blinks at me. "*What*?"

"What? I just watched *Silence of the Lambs* for the first time last night. I don't wanna be sacrificed."

"I genuinely can't tell if you're being serious or not right now."

I giggle. "Good."

Noah shakes his head, dropping the topic entirely, and drags us both up the driveway to the front door.

His white T-shirt clings to his muscular back, and I swear that I start drooling. I push those thoughts away, though. He's been acting far too strange today, and mauling him in front of his stepdad probably won't help that.

As soon as we step into the house, the sound of music and voices crowd me. There are way too many people here for my liking, and even worse than that... there's *children*. I turn to Noah, horrified. "Isn't this a birthday party? Why are there kids?"

He shrugs. "He actually hates his birthday. Says it makes him feel lonely instead of loved. So, he makes it a neighborhood pool party. But *I* call it his birthday party."

I stare at him blankly. "You brought me to a pool party with no bathing suit?"

Noah winks and drags me onto the back patio. I drop the cheesy birthday card I bought on the gift table, forcing my short legs to move faster. "I prefer swimming without them anyway," he says.

Sweet baby Jesus.

As soon as we make it to the pool, Noah gets to one knee before me. My eyes nearly pop out of my head as I stare down at him. Before I can say anything or look at anyone though, he puts one of my feet on his knee and starts unlacing my sandals. He kisses my calf once before moving onto the next foot. Once he's done, he pats the ground and looks at the pool. "Enjoy it for a second. Lets you avoid all the strangers while I go find the grumpy bastard."

I look at the pool and immediately sit down, tossing my legs into the cold water. "You don't have to tell me twice."

Laughing, he turns and runs back into the house. While he's gone, I can't help but marvel at the structure of the home behind me. It literally screams money and confidence.

And for his stepdad to come from the military?

I'm telling Aiden and Casey to leave as soon as they fucking can.

There's always such a stigma that the military can ruin you the second you leave—either from lack of other work experience or trauma. And this is just proof that that verdict isn't always the case.

After a few minutes, I hear Noah's voice on the patio again, and I lift my legs up to stand. A hand appears next to me seconds later, with a deep voice saying, "Allow me."

My eyes pinch together at the sound of that voice, forcing me to hesitate.

I know that voice...

My heart sinks at the realization.

No fucking way.

Looking up slowly, I'm met with brown boots,

blue jeans, and a brown button-down shirt rolled up to his elbows.

Those tattoos...

With his hand still extended out, my heart stills inside of my chest entirely, just as Noah says, "Sean, this is Lauren, my girlfriend. Lauren, this is my friend and once-upon-a-time stepdad, Sean Calloway."

And Sean stares me dead in the eyes, equally horrified.

FIVE

LAUREN.

My Lauren.

My Lauren…who is also…Noah's Lauren.

The words fly out of my mouth before I can stop them. "Fuck me."

The words must short-circuit Lauren out of her own shock because she takes my hand and jumps up to her feet, staring at Noah as she says, "Sean."

Noah's head swivels back and forth between the two of us, confusion lining every feature of his face. "Do you two know each other?"

"No!" Lauren says, at the exact same time that I say, "Yes."

Noah pauses. "Which one is it?"

My eyes sweep down her body from head to toe.

This is undoubtedly my Lauren. Just with new hair.

I raise an eyebrow at her when she looks back at me like a deer caught in headlights. Her skin is a white as a ghost, which says more than enough considering she was summer-tanned mere seconds ago. Her voice shakes as she responds. "We sorta, *kinda* know each other."

Now both of my eyebrows raise as I stare down at her. "So much for that deal of always saying the truth when we're in each other's presence."

Her eyes nearly pop out of her head at those words. Almost as if they were the final confirmation that she's well and truly *fucked*. Noah turns his attention from the both of us, solely to her. "Okay, what's going on? How do you know Sean? What deal is he talking about?"

Almost as if she has the ability to turn blinders on, she chews on her bottom lip and pretends I don't exist at all. She turns to Noah, saying, "Is there somewhere we can talk? Please?"

It pisses me the fuck off.

One night *changed* me. I didn't even know that was possible. I've been searching for this girl for over a year now—refusing to date or fuck anyone else—and now, she's ignoring me entirely.

Whilst dating my goddamned stepson.

What a cosmic fucking joke.

I've never seen Noah look so confused, but he simply takes her hand and leads them into the house. And I'm left standing here, jointly wondering what the fuck I'm going to do.

NOAH

Out of my dozens of potential outcomes, I didn't see this one coming.

And I don't even truly know how to feel about it.

I run one of my hands through my hair. I don't know if I've ever felt more stress in my life. I turn to Lauren as she sits crisscross on my childhood bed.

"So, you and Sean...fucked...before you met me."

She's sawing at her bottom lip again. "Yes."

"And you didn't know we were close or anything?"

Her head shake is firm. "I would take a lie detector test right now if I could. I haven't seen him in over a year."

I turn to look back outside the window overlooking the pool, scanning for the man of the hour. Ever since we left to talk, the party has dwindled significantly, and I'm both thankful *and* bummed. I didn't want to ruin the man's birthday, but I also couldn't let whatever was about to unfold spiral out of control. I swallow roughly as I ask my next question. "Do...did he tell you? About us? And sharing?"

His answer is a quiet whisper. "Yes."

My eyes close.

Goddamn it.

No wonder she turned white with anxiety. Not only was she panicking about seeing a one-night stand —that happened to be my stepdad—but she probably thought she walked into a threesome with zero consent.

I don't even have the courage to look back at her when I respond. "Do you think it's gross?"

Lauren chokes on a laugh. "I literally just told you that I fucked him through a glory hole, and you're asking me if I find you *gross*? Don't you think you should be repulsed by *me* instead? I'm waiting to get dumped right now."

Jesus Christ.

I don't know whether to be extremely turned on right now or even more nervous. But this is something I need to know. "Answer the question, please."

I jump when her arms snake around my waist. I didn't even know she got up. She presses her nose into the middle of my back, nuzzling into my warmth. Regardless of the plethora of thoughts swarming through my brain, it makes me relax, and I grip one of her hands as she responds. "No, Noah. I don't think it's gross. Everyone is consenting adults, and people like what they like. It's not like the man raised you."

I nod my head.

I needed to hear that.

She hesitates before asking, "Have you two been together while we've been seeing each other, though?"

I'm instantly shaking my head. I turn around to face her, cupping her heart-shaped face in my hands. My words are raw. "Absolutely not. It's just been us. And frankly, I think I'm starting to fall in love with you. But I won't lie that...it's been a want, sure. But no, no cheating."

Her lower lip wobbles. "You love me?"

"I do. You make me happy."

"But...?"

"But...this is what I like. This is what makes me happy. This is what makes *us* happy. One woman, just for us. Sexually, romantically. Exclusive. That's why I've been so on edge today. I knew this would come out, somehow. I just didn't think it would happen like *this*, with there already being history."

She makes a little scoffing sound as if to say *no shit*, and it makes me smile. "Yeah, I kinda pieced that part together."

Now it's my turn to make that odd sound. "So...?"

She instantly knows what I'm questioning. "I've never done the whole sharing thing, outside of just sex. I don't really know how it works."

I feel guilty for the hope that blooms through me.

She's not running for the hills, at least.

Lauren continues. "But I'm willing to try. As long as he doesn't despise my existence."

I shake my head. "Believe me. He's told me for literally a year now how he didn't know if he could share again...because he may have found the one."

Her eyebrows rise in shock. "The *one*?"

Deciding to pull a fuck-it moment, I lean down and pick her up, carrying her to the bed. She lets out the cutest sound of surprise, and when we land on my bed, I make her straddle my lap. "Mhhm. I was jealous every single time he brought it up. How could I not be? We would fool around sometimes. And I kept wanting to know what was so special about this girl. I wanted to experienced that."

My eyes roll when Lauren settles her weight down on me entirely, and as luck would fucking have it, grinds against the boner I've been fighting. A grunt leaves me as she says, "Well, now that you know who she is, what do you think?"

"I think I understand why he's been so ruined."

Her eyes line with tears.

I don't know everything about her past yet, but I

know more than enough to conclude that she's never felt genuinely loved.

And fuck, if I don't want to change that.

With Sean.

Moving my hands to unbutton her shorts, I hiss out another breath when she grinds into my cock again. "But I regret to inform you both that I need you one more time before we face whatever conversation this will be."

A giggle leaves her, turning into a moan when I grind up into her. A part of me actually hopes Sean is standing outside the door right now, but I push the thought away anyway.

We have one main rule—no toxicity.

Lauren can't be any different.

But as she gets up and peels off her clothes, straddling me again stark naked, I ask—more like demand—the one question that's been turning me on for hours now. I tug a piece of her white hair, forcing her down to me as I growl out, "Fuck me while you tell me what my stepdad did to you."

"FUCK," I grunt out as I pump my cock with my fist. "*Fuck me.*"

Laying on my bed, jerking off, and daydreaming about when I met Lauren for the millionth time definitely wasn't on my to-do list for the day, but I know I won't be able to face either one of them if I'm hung-up and edged.

Even if I've masturbated to the thought of her more times than I can count.

1.5 YEARS AGO

After making my way back to my truck, room booked for the morning ahead, I stop short when I see Lauren standing outside of it.

Oh, no. That's not gonna work.

Making my way to her, I place my hands on my hips as I stare down at her with a raised brow, easily towering over her as I stand at six-three. "Who opened the door for you?"

She looks around the very empty parking lot, confused. "Me?"

"Uh-uh," I tsk, opening the truck door. "Get in."

She stares at me, trying to read me.

I give her absolutely nothing.

Sighing tiredly, she climbs back in the black truck. I close the door and count to five before opening it again, smiling. "C'mon, sweetheart."

She gives me a deadpan stare. "You're kidding, right?"

"Do I look like I am?"

I'm met with an exaggerated eye roll as she gets out of the truck again. "Thanks, *Daddy*. I feel babied."

Fuck.

I'm instantly hard as a rock. New kink, unlocked.

I always tried to steer clear of that one—knowing

damn well how bad a Daddy kink could look while having threesomes with my stepson—but it sounds way too fucking good coming from her lips.

Before she can blink, I'm slamming the door shut, picking her up, and wrapping her legs around my waist so we're eye level, forcing my mouth on hers. She moans into me as she melts against the truck door behind her, and the sound sends lightning bolts directly to my dick. I pull away, panting. "Call me that again."

Her eyes are dazed. "Daddy."

I need us to get the fuck out of this parking lot before I come in my jeans.

Carrying her around the building, I see the infamous entrance to the glory hole one of Noah's friends told me about after far too many Jägerbombs. It's covered in graffiti, and if you didn't know any better, would probably look like the entrance to an abandoned house.

Testing the knob with Lauren still in my arms, I almost want to shout with joy when it gives in immediately. And as soon as you walk in, you're there. It's the size of a janitor's closet, cut in half with a piece of drywall in the middle to separate sides, and a wide circle cut in the middle.

The logical part of my brain knows this once was a

genuine janitor's closet that had a pipe going through it.

But who gives a shit now?

I turn around, shut the door, and lock it.

Setting Lauren down, I smooth back her hair as I ask one final time. "You want this?"

She nods her head fast, eager.

I stare at her, amazed.

What a fucking woman.

Before I can say anything else, she gets on one side of the drywall and kneels. I'm more than thankful that her dress covers her knees—only imagining the amount of fluids and grime beneath us—but I push the thought away as I move toward the other side of the wall. Unbuckling my belt and moving the zipper down on my jeans, I take my cock out and pump it with my fist. I spit down at it, loudly, and I hear a whimper on the other side of the wall.

Taking a deep breath, I stop teasing myself and stick my dick through the wall. "Suck Daddy's cock, little girl."

I barely get to finish my sentence. Her mouth wraps around my flesh, sucking and swallowing all seven inches instantly. She wretches as it hits the back of her throat, and my mouth drops open as a gurgled moan leaves me. "Oh, *my fuck!*"

She moans, sending vibrations up my dick and down my spine, and I instantly wish I had something to hold onto.

There's hardly any more talking. She continues bobbing her head up and down the length of my cock, and I swear that I'm in fucking Heaven. Or Hell. The current scenario fits both. Moans and grunts leave me, and as she reaches one hand through the hole to fondle my balls, I know I'm about to lose my goddamn mind.

"Lauren," I pant. "Sweetheart, I'm gonna come soon."

She pulls back, and for the slightest second, I almost feel disappointment. I would have loved to shoot my cum down her throat, but I know that I'm a stranger and that's a major ris—

The thought flies straight out of my mind when I feel her rub the tip of my cock over her pussy lips. Seconds later, she's thrusting herself back against the hole, and my dick is fully seated in her wet cunt.

"Holy shit!" I roar.

"Daddy," she moans. "Oh my God, yes."

My dick actually twitches inside of her. "Lauren, I can't. We shouldn't..."

She ignores me, thrusting back against me again and again.

She's fucking herself on my dick.

If I am in Heaven, I'm going straight to Hell.

Gritting my teeth, I growl out my next words, giving in. "Are you on birth control? I don't have a condom."

She moans before responding, "I can't get pregnant."

My jaw ticks. We're talking about that afterwards because I will be fucking damned if I become a dad at the age of forty-five.

Absolutely not.

For now, though, I just accept what is.

Thrusting my hips into her this time, I pretty much fight the demons keeping my orgasm at bay. "Rub your clit, little girl."

I can't see if she is, but instantly, her pussy becomes a Vise-Grip on me. She cries out, "Fuck, I'm gonna come! I'm gonna come, Daddy. *Daddy*!"

The groan that leaves my lips is almost painful as her orgasm milks mine right out of me. "*Laurennnn*!"

I breed my little girl for the first time, right here, at a fucking glory hole. My dick pulses inside of her, shooting load after load of cum. By the time I'm finished, shaking and whipped, Lauren laughs.

I pant. "What?"

The laugh is almost hysterical. "How am I supposed to say goodbye to you after that?"

And I'm left thinking the exact same thing.

PRESENT DAY

My fist moves up and down my length erratically as the memory of her pussy milking me hits me. I tighten my fist, and it's seconds later before I'm blowing my load all over my stomach, biting my lip to stifle my moans. My cock jerks and twitches as cum spirts out, covering me, and I swear it's a hard enough orgasm that some of it hits my fucking beard.

Exhausted, I lay there, staring at the ceiling.

That night after we finished, we rented a hotel room at another place that *didn't* look cockroach infested, and instantly fell asleep.

By the time I woke up, she was gone.

No goodbye. No note. Nothing.

Every single fucking time a blonde woman walked in my bar, I thought it was her. I kept getting my hopes up, hoping to at least talk to her one more time. Even if nothing else happened, she intrigued me far before we had sex.

Now I wonder if I was looking for the wrong girl the entire time. How amiss I was to look for just hair color, as if that couldn't be changed. She was literally in a dress that night. I should've looked for the tattoos. *Something.*

It doesn't matter now, though. Because she's in my fucking house.

And as my dick gets hard again at the realization, I come to the conclusion:

I'm not letting her leave again.

Lauren belongs to me and Noah, both.

SEVEN

NOAH LAYS NEXT TO ME, snoring lightly, and I stare at him full of complete and utter envy. How he can sleep so peacefully when there's so much still unknown is completely and utterly wild to me.

Men.

Looking over at the clock on his nightstand, I sigh when I see the time stamp of 1:10 AM staring back at me.

I feel completely and utterly wired.

Getting up, I pad to the patio quietly, aiming directly for the pool. While I didn't see Sean again tonight—him claiming some bullshit excuse that he didn't feel well so his guests would leave—I highly doubt he would put his foot down at me swimming in his pool.

If he wanted me out that bad, he'd just kick me out.

The thought makes me pause as I shimmy out of my crop top and shorts. *God, I hope he doesn't hate me.* Pushing the thought away and using my lingerie as my bathing suit, I jump in the water, submerging myself instantly.

Bad idea, my subconscious screams. I pop out of the water with a gasp, shivering instantly. I thought the pool would have kept some of its warmth from earlier that day, but apparently the pool's heater isn't on.

I jump and turn towards the patio door when I hear it slide open and a man cursing. Sean looks at me, bewilderment clear on his face. "What the fuck are you doing?"

I point out the obvious. "Swimming?"

He glares at me before stomping over to a thermostat near the sliding glass doors. "It's fucking freezing. Are you trying to get sick?"

"I thought it would have been warm from earlier today," I whine through chattering teeth.

He merely shakes his head at me, pressing buttons and grumbling under his breath. The sight makes me want to giggle, but I have the feeling that I'll be scolded even more if I do.

He turns back towards me, walking my way, only

to collapse against a patio chair. "The pool heater is now on overdrive. You should warm up soon."

"Sorry..."

Sean lifts his head to look at me. "For?"

I think about it for a second before saying, "Yes."

A chuckle leaves him and he goes back to laying flat, staring up at the sky. Deciding to join him, since he joined me, I turn to float on my back. I know without a doubt in my mind that my nipples are pebbled underneath my bra...but I just hope he keeps his eyes on the sky.

While I would have thought otherwise, the silence between us is nice. Comfortable.

Different.

It's the laying still that makes me uneasy.

Moving my arms backwards, I glide through the water, keeping my eyes up. Though, the sound of the water splashing must snap him out of whatever trance we was in. "You swim?"

"Mhhhmm. It was my escape in high school and college. It's the only way I got into college, actually."

"What did you go to college for?"

"Marketing and advertisement."

"What do you do now?"

I smile as I move to flip over and swim towards the edge of the pool where he's sitting. "Are we playing the question game again, Sean?"

His gaze is heavy on me. "I tried looking for you, you know."

The smile on my face drops with shock following it. "What? Why? Why didn't you just call me?"

A look of pure confusion and sarcasm falls over him. "With what phone number? 1-800-find-your-hookup?"

I bark out a laugh. His lips turn up at the sound, his gaze dropping to my mouth, but he doesn't comment. I sober up instantly. "I left my phone number on the key card holder the receptionist gave us. You really didn't see it?"

Instantly, his face falls, and I know he's telling the truth. "No. I...I was really upset there wasn't a note or anything. Pretty much threw the key card at the recep-tionist before I left."

I cringe.

I really hope that wasn't Rory.

"I couldn't find a piece of paper. Couldn't even find a napkin. Was severely late for work—almost lost my job entirely that day, actually—and you were in a coma. Tried to do what I could."

Sean wipes a heavy hand over his face tiredly, saying, "Fuck," loudly.

I flinch back.

His voice is hoarse. "I'm sorry, just...frustrated.

Looked for you for an entire year, you know. Kept thinking you'd come to the bar again."

One of my eyebrows raise in question. "Would you go into the bar of a man you fucked at a glory-hole if he didn't call you back when you did, indeed, leave a number? I wasn't going to stalk you, Sean." My voice drops down into a whisper. "For fuck's sake, I already felt like a cheap whore when I woke up."

He sits up ramrod straight and grips the chair. My eyes immediately land on his tanned, tattooed arms. "You are *not* a whore."

I break my gaze from his arms. "I'm literally eye-fucking you right now."

"Yeah, and I have been the second you jumped in that damn pool. What does that make me?"

Fair point.

Hard to not look at someone so intensely when something so intimate was shared.

I shrug. "Point still stands. I was a hook-up at a glory-hole. Me trying to find you, especially after you didn't call, would have landed me with a restraining order in a lot of books."

"I thought it was the sharing scenario that scared you off. Since I told you that it would just be one-on-one that night."

I tilt my head back and forth, dipping my hair back into the water. "I'm still here, aren't I?"

He blinks in confusion. "What do you mean?"

"I mean, you told me that night, and Noah told me again this afternoon—and I'm still here, aren't I?" I smirk, and my eyes watch as he swallows roughly. The poor man. "I'm a grown woman, Sean. If I didn't want to be in either yours or Noah's presence with the information presented, then I wouldn't be here."

He stands then, and I hardly have a moment to blink before he's right in front of me. "I want to kiss you so badly right now."

It's Noah's voice that breaks us apart. My head snaps to the patio entrance where he stands, arms crossed and eyes hungry. "Do it, then," he says.

Sean looks between the both of us. "If we do this, then that's it. I'm not trying again."

Noah raises an eyebrow. "I know. She does, too."

Sean looks at me then. "You do?"

I nod. "I told him everything. Every single detail. And he told me both of yours in return."

Noah speaks up again. "She's our girl, romantically and sexually. She wants some time getting used to it, but she wants this. She wants us."

Sean looks at me for confirmation.

I nod. "Just my Daddy and my boyfriend. Yours."

EIGHT

"JESUS, FUCK," Sean says, standing up straight. He lifts his t-shirt up and over his head before dropping his shorts and splashing into the pool before either Lauren or myself can form another sentence. I know without a doubt in my mind that he's still holding back—but I also know he's going to break.

And I'm going to break right along with him.

I follow suite and uncross my arms, getting undressed as I watch Sean nearly maul Lauren. His mouth covers hers, tongues twisting and swiping at the other, all while her hands trail down to his abs and waist.

Watching her enjoy this, knowing I'm watching, has me hard in an instant. I don't keeping my boxers on like Sean did, though. I kick them to the side and wrap a hand around my length, jerking off as I step closer to them.

A part of me is content watching them have fun.

The other part of me wants to see just how much cock our girl can take, and hopefully take some myself.

As Sean pulls away from Lauren and promptly lifts her up, out of the water and onto the concrete edge—I fully know it's the other part of me that's going to win tonight.

Because fuck, she's hot.

Lauren whines. "That...you...you know that saying, 'I couldn't lift her soaking wet,' I never thought I'd be the test."

Sean smirks up at her. "Do I need to remind you that you're in the presence of two men who are quite literally conditioned to be fit and ruthless?"

I laugh as I step closer. "I think she does. I bet if you peel those panties off her, she'll be soaking wet in an entirely different way."

Sean looks up at me with a smirk. "Good idea."

My mouth salivates as I watch him toy with her lace panties. Lauren goes to lift her hips but he measly tsks at her before ripping them entirely. The material falls to the concrete as Lauren gasps, "Hey! I liked those."

Sean lifts one of her legs up and onto his shoulders.

"And I never want to see a pair of panties on you again. Understand me?"

Lauren swallows and nods timidly.

Finally getting close enough to stand behind Lauren, I tug at her wet hair, forcing her neck to crane back. Her gaze lands directly on my cock, and I swear that a bead of pre-cum forms on the tip under her attention. "We believe in using our words here, baby girl."

Her eyes glide up to meet mine. "Yes, sir."

A yelp flies out of her next, and I smirk when I peer down to see Sean fully biting into her inner thigh. Her hand flies to his hair, trying to push him away, and it only makes him bite her harder. Finally, he releases, only to scoot her even closer to him. "*I'm* the one who asked if you understood me, little girl."

Her chest heaves. "Yes, Daddy."

He smiles then. "Good girl. Now, suck your boyfriend's cock while I taste this cunt. Can't leave him out. Told you—we're a package deal."

I don't even give her a chance to respond. I've been wanting to shove my length into her mouth since Sean lifted her out of the pool, and the second she turns her head toward me, I do just that. She moans loudly against me, and I look down again, right when I see Sean lick up her slit.

I can't help the pride in my tone. "She tastes amazing, doesn't she?"

"Fucking incredible," he responds, following his words with more swipes of his tongue. He lifts her other leg to his shoulder, bending it slightly to spread her even further. She cries out against my length when he sticks his pointer finger inside of her, curling it.

"Yeah, baby?" I ask, grunting and piling her wet hair into a makeshift ponytail. "You like Sean licking your sweet little pussy while I fuck this pretty face? I bet you'd love seeing him fuck mine, wouldn't you?"

She moans in response, sucking me further into her mouth.

Sean breaks apart to talk, even as he adds another finger to the mix. His other hand wraps around Lauren's back, unclipping her bra in seconds, and we both groan at the sight of her tits dropping free. I reach down to grab one as Sean grabs the other, twisting her nipple. Her eyes practically cross when I talk again. "Hey, Sean. You know Lauren's a squirter, right?"

He looks up at me. "Excuse me?"

I jut my chin down to her pussy. "Test it. See if I'm lying."

He growls. "Should have brought her over sooner. Killing me."

Lauren pops her mouth off of me with a shout as Sean inserts a third finger, curling it with the others as he thrusts in and out of her, hard. "Oh my God, oh my God, oh my God!"

I yank her hair back towards me. "I'm not done with you, baby girl. Suck my cock. You can squirt and suck, can't you? Or do you need me to use you like a fleshlight?"

Her mouth goes slack, either in pleasure or shock, and I take that as my answer. Repositioning myself, I hold her hair with both hands now and thrust in and out of her mouth fast—properly fucking her throat. Drool slides down her chin with tears from her eyes, and gags are quick to follow.

Sean groans. "She's so fucking pretty. You're so fucking beautiful, Lauren."

Lauren moans loudly. Sean laughs, using more force to finger-fuck her, and I groan with her as I watch her tits bounce from the force of it. "She got so fucking tight just then."

I growl. "Yeah? You need some praise from your boyfriend and Daddy, sweetheart? Is that what gets you off? Being our little praise-slut? You don't even have to talk for me to know that."

Sean hums in agreement as he goes back down to swiper his tongue at her clit. "I agree. Pussy talks for itself."

As I hit the back of Lauren's throat again, my lower stomach clenches. I grunt as I pull out of her mouth, not wanting to blow my load too soon. I keep my hold on her hair though and crane her neck up so she can meet my gaze. "Look at me when he makes you come."

She nods furiously. "I'm so close."

I smirk and turn to Sean. "You hear that? She's *so* close. The poor baby."

Lauren keeps her eyes on mine, and I watch as her body go as tight as a bowstring. When her eyes roll into the back of her head, I look down at her cunt and watch as she squirts over Sean's fingers. Sean curses under breath and watches, memorized.

"Good fucking girl," I praise. "Squirt on him for me, baby. So fucking pretty for us."

Her moans are a mix of broken up words and noises, and it's the most erotic thing I've ever seen in my life. Eventually, her breaths come out slow and deep, and Sean breaks apart from her. Satisfaction lines every feature on him, and I know I'm no different.

I let go of Lauren's hair, petting it down softly. "Good girl."

She whimpers one word that nearly makes my knees buckle.

"More."

NINE

WATER DRIPS from my body as Noah carries me into the house with Sean quick on our heels. I laugh, the slightest bit delirious as I look back at him. "Sorry about your floor."

His eyebrows raise in an expression that clearly says *you're shitting me, right?* And it only makes me laugh harder.

Noah shakes his head. "He's giving you the *dad* look, isn't he?"

"Yup."

Noah turns to Sean. "No *dad* looks before sex."

Sean turns *the dad look* to Noah, forcing an obnoxious laugh from both of us. Now it's Sean's turn to shake his head.

If there was ever a time for a *like father, like son,* moment, it would be now.

As Noah carries me into his room, I'm all but thrown onto the bed, and I lean up on my elbows to stare at the men before me. "Why this room?"

Sean stalks up to me, smirking. "We're wet. And you're a squirter. One bed to ruin you in, the other bed to sleep in."

I look between them. "You two sleep in the same bed?"

Noah kneels down on the bed, nearly crawling to me. My eyes drop to his length, and an ache forms inside of me all over again. It only grows when I drop my eyes to Sean's wet boxers, finding him equally as hard. "We go wherever our girl goes."

I swallow hard. "So...so this is well and truly just about...me? Nothing between either of you?"

Noah closes the distance between us, placing a soft kiss on my lips. "Just about you. It's not like that. Sure, if we touch from some positions or actions, then we touch. But all pleasure and happiness stems from you."

I look back at Sean. He nods, peeling his boxers down slowly. My mouth goes dry when I see his cock, heavy and hard. "Just you, sweetheart. But don't think we're not both going to fuck you at the same time, either."

My mouth drops. "What?"

Noah chuckles darkly then. "You heard him."

I turn to look at him with wide eyes. "Like...like both in...one?"

Sean steps closer to the bed, his eyes dark and heavy. "Both in one. Have you ever done that before?"

I shake my head nervously. The smile on his face is utterly wicked. "Looks like I get to be *two* of your firsts then. Now, open up this pretty little mouth. I've missed it." He turns his gaze to Noah. "Go in my room and get a toy. We need to get her pussy adjusted before she can take both of us."

Jesus Christ. What did I get myself into?

Noah presses a kiss to my lips again before he's up and out of the room.

Leaving Sean and I alone.

TEN

"LAY DOWN on your stomach and open up, sweetheart," I say, stepping to the edge of the bed. "Been far too long since I've had a mouth around me, and you don't even know how happy I am that it's yours."

Lauren follows my directions instantly, and pure pride spreads through my chest. She wraps one of her hands around my length, forcing a hiss out of my mouth. "How long has it been?"

"A year and a half."

Her eyes snap up to mine. "You're lying."

Just like Noah did outside, I gather her hair up and out of her face. "Why would I lie? We have a deal, remember?"

"You haven't been with anyone else since me? Not even Noah?"

"Mm-mhm," I hum, shaking my head. "You know how you said you're a grown woman, outside?"

"Yeah…"

"Well, sweetheart, I'm a grown man who has tattoos older than you. I know how to be patient. But I can tell you that my patience is running thin this very second. So while I love the sound of your voice, I'm going to need you to suck Daddy's cock now."

A whimper comes out of her mouth as I slide my cock in. The tension immediately leaves my shoulders as a sigh of relief hits me. I pull her hair, bringing her closer to me, and groan unbelievably loud when her nose hits my stomach. Pulling out the slightest bit, I let her take in a deep breath before I do it again, reveling in the feel of her throat constricting around me.

"God," I moan. "I've missed this fucking mouth. You know I've jerked off almost every day, thinking about it?"

The revelation makes her moan.

I hope she knows it really is the truth.

Finally, Noah strides back into the room—still naked.

Pressing Lauren's nose to my stomach again, moaning when she gags around me, I look down to the toys in his hands. "What'd you pick?"

He holds up one small toy, normally meant for anal, and a pink vibrator. "I'm going to fuck her with this in, and this is to make sure cum so hard that she cries."

His elaboration makes me laugh—though it only turns into a moan when Lauren swipes a hand up and tugs on my balls. I look down at her, amused when I find her eyes in a pout. "Don't get bratty with me, little girl. Keep going. Unless you want Noah to join you?"

Her eyes slide to him, and she nods.

I look at him and gesture to the floor. He gets to his knees immediately, placing the toys on the bed. "You heard her. Just for a second, though. Tonight is about her. You'll earn your turn."

Instead of waiting for me to take my cock out of her mouth, he immediately goes to sucking on my balls, and I fight demons to not blow here and now. His hand moves around, cupping my ass, and I have to bite my tongue for some balance of pain when I feel one of his fingers teasing my asshole.

I move all of Lauren's hair to one hand and use my free one to stroke Noah's head. "Both of my little ones like sucking Daddy, huh?" I growl out.

Noah's eyes fly up to mine, his mouth still sucking my flesh into his mouth.

I read it as clear as day.

He likes the Daddy title.

Oh, how fun.

I grip him by the hair, needing to test it. Moving him off me, I push the words out. "Open your mouth so Daddy can spit in it. Then go take care of our girl."

The man opens his mouth without hesitation, as if I have a gun to his head.

Apparently, I was dead-fucking wrong thinking he would find it gross.

I slowly spit in his mouth and watch him swallow it. My dick twitches inside of Lauren's throat.

We have all the time in the world, I remind myself. *Don't come yet.*

The thought makes me gesture Noah to the bed.

And he doesn't wait. He gets on the bed, sitting right behind Lauren, and spreads her legs. Her eyes go down as he trails his hands up the back of her thighs, and I know she would turn around if she had the chance.

So, I give it to her.

This time.

Pulling out of her mouth, I flip her onto her back. She gasps at the change, and I take that as my opening to slide my cock right back in. In this position, it slides straight down her throat with little resistance, bringing a growl out of my chest.

I look at Noah right as he slides the smallest toy into Lauren, and the moan she lets out sends lightning right through me.

I already know I'm going to bust down her pretty little throat. But I talk to her anyway, even if it might make me bust. "You gonna let your boyfriend fuck you, baby? While I'm down your throat?"

She moans in response.

I don't even know if she knows there's a toy inside of her. It's the size of one or two of my fingers, and with her being as brainless as she is right now, she could think it is one of our hands playing with her.

"Hand me the vibrator," I say to Noah. "Then fuck our girl."

In seconds, the vibrator is powered on in my hands, and he's positioned over top of her, showing just how eager he really is. Noah goes slow, pressing his weight down into her. Lauren spreads her legs even wider, feeling him, and fuck if I want nothing else than to ruin her.

"You want us to ruin you, baby? You want to be our praise slut and take both of our cocks in that pussy?"

Another gurgled moan.

And it nearly turns into a scream on my cock when Noah thrusts inside of her entirely, aligned right against the toy. Noah clenches his teeth hard enough that I'm surprised he doesn't break one, his eyes rolling. "So. Fucking. Tight."

I take that as my cue to put the vibrator directly on Lauren's swollen clit, shifting my hips to thrust my cock as far down her throat as she can take.

Instantaneously, her legs begin to shake and Noah's breathing becomes erratic. "Fuck, she's coming already. Fuck. Sean...I can't."

God.

Yeah.

She's never leaving us.

I'll hold her fucking hostage if I have to.

Lauren moan gurgles around me. Deciding to give her a reprieve, I take myself out of her mouth while keeping the vibrator pressed against her. "You coming on his cock, little girl?"

"Yes! Noah! Sean! Yes, *fuck*!"

"Lauren," Noah grunts out. "Take my cum, baby. Oh, take all that cum. Fucking milk me."

I watch them both lose it, stroking myself up and down as they shake and moan uncontrollably as one. Pleasure meeting pleasure, moan meeting moan.

When both of them collapse, I only smile.

"Hope you can get hard again." I smirk. "Because now she's going to take both of our cocks."

Noah pulls out of Lauren as she stares up at the ceiling in a daze. I chuckle when I see him still hard as granite. He smirks back at me, wrapping a hand around his length. "Believe me. We're not gonna have a problem there."

ELEVEN

IT'S TAKES only seconds to reposition Lauren between Sean and I. I'm laying flat on my back with her back to my chest. My cock is already nestled inside of Lauren—making my life hard enough as I fight tooth and nail to not come already—with Sean teasing his cock over her pussy.

He looks right at her. "Tell me you want this."

She doesn't hesitate. "I want this."

I reassure her anyway. "We don't have to, baby. We have all the time in the world. I know we jumped into the deep end, but if you don't want to, then we don't have to."

Her words turn firm. "You want to own me? Prove it."

I scoff out a laugh at the bratty attitude. My hands come up to grip her waist tightly, probably hard enough to leave bruises, as I lower my mouth to nip at her ear.

She shudders at the sensation, paired with Sean spreading her legs and staring directly at her pussy. His eyes are dark and hungry. "You told me a year ago that you couldn't have kids. What did you mean by that?"

I pick my head up to look at him. "She never told you?"

Lauren laughs. "We didn't get there yet."

My eyes pinch. "But you...?"

Sean goes to open his mouth, but Lauren talks before he can try. "It was literally a glory hole at four in the morning. Logical thinking wasn't present." She turns her gaze back to him. "I had my tubes tied when I was twenty-one."

His eyes fill with questions but he doesn't press it.

Thank fuck.

So not the time.

Instead, he crawls up the bed and looks down at us both. Like a switch is flipped, his dominant personality overtakes his curious and gentle one. "Then we're both going to breed this fucking pussy at the same time. Think you can handle that?"

She doesn't even get a chance to nod her head

before Sean is pressing against her, forcing his length into her pussy—right alongside me. My grip on Lauren's waist goes even tighter at the sensation.

Lauren cries out. "Sean!"

Sean pauses. "You okay?"

Her head nod is fast and eager, even as her breath comes out in pants. "Don't stop. Just so...*full*."

Sean groans and raises his arm. At first, I think he's going to swat one of mine away and grip her chest, but he does something else entirely. He wraps a hand around her throat and picks her head up from my shoulder, whispering. "No brain-dead praise-slut here. You look at Daddy when there are two cocks inside of you."

Her mouth drops open at the words and sensation. And, of-fucking-course, Sean fucking spits inside of it, right as he bottoms out his entire length inside of her.

All of us pause, adjusting.

I breathe in deeply, trying not to lose it. With his full weight pressed against the both of us, I actually fucking whimper the words, "Sean. Move."

He listens, slowly withdraws while keeping his focus entirely on her, his hand still on her throat, and thrusts right back in, analyzing every single reaction and emotion she could possibly have. Lauren cries out, her moan rough on her vocal cords, and I do the exact same.

The motions repeat more times than I can count as we all get adjusted. And as we do, I'm hit with a deep realization.

How I love Lauren.

How I love Sean.

How I never want to give this up.

How I know this is wrong, but it feels so goddamn right.

Deciding to take a risk, I manage to say, "Lauren?"

Sean releases her throat long enough for her to answer. "Ye-yeah?"

I look at him as I lay my feet flat on the bed, getting ready to thrust into her myself. Her skin is sweaty between us, and I know that the time for being gentle is quickly running out. "For what it's worth...you're our first doing this with, too."

And then I thrust up into her.

Right as Sean goes back to choking her with a fervor.

Her entire body shakes from the force of the thrust, a harsh scream coming out of her mouth. I do it again. Twice. Three times. I lose count of the amount of times I thrust up into her, stretching and ruining her for anyone else, all while rubbing against Sean's cock inside of her. Her tits bounce with every thrust, and if I weren't scared of blowing my load inside of her at the snap of my fingers, I'd be ruining them just as much as we're ruining her cunt.

Looking up at Sean, I goad him. "What? Not going to fuck her, too? I thought she was *our* girl?"

Lauren cries out.

Sean hisses, "I was trying not to break her."

I thrust in harder than ever. Sean shudders, and I know I must have hit a sensitive spot of him, too. "She can take it. Now fuck our girl so she's ruined for anyone else."

He shakes his head but pulls out the moment I go in, fucking her in tandem with me. Every time I pull out, he's thrusting in. Our cocks rub together with every motion, adding to the sensation of it all, and I feel my balls start to draw up as the minutes go by.

I groan out the words, "I'm gonna come. I need to come."

"Me too. I'm right there," Sean says.

Lauren whines loudly. "Please!"

That's all I needed to hear. I give one last, final thrust into her before my cock is twitching and my orgasm wracks through me. Fire lights me up from the inside out as I come inside of her, unable to even speak. Sean follows immediately after, stilling inside of her as his dick twitches against mine. He groans, keeping his grip on her throat in a possessive hold, maintaining eye contact as we fill her up.

Minutes pass. We all stay stock still, riding the wave of pleasure that's crashed over us all. Sweat coats each of us as our exhaustion sets in.

Sean pulls out first, sighing. As gently as I can, I follow suit.

He speaks first. "C'mon. Shower time."

PRINCESS TREATMENT DURING THE DAY? Immaculate experience.

Princess treatment at night? Equally fantastic.

But princess treatment after you've just been ruined? The best thing to ever happen.

Even if it's a first for me.

Post-shower and hair scrubbing to get the smell of chlorine and sex off of me, I lay in a crumpled ball in one of Sean's T-shirts and boxers, staring up at the ceiling of his bedroom—more exhausted than I have ever been in my entire life. Sean and Noah both lay on their sides next to me, watching me.

I give each of them a side-long glance. "I'm not gonna break into a million pieces, ya know."

Sean moves his head from side to side. "You could."

Noah slyly moves a hand down my stomach. "You know, you didn't at the end. We can fix that now."

I swat his hand away. "Okay, I might not break into a million pieces, but she absolutely will."

Sean bursts out laughing. "*She?*"

"Would you prefer I call it a he?"

Noah's head collapses on my shoulder. "Okay, both of you. No more. Stop talking. I take it back."

Sean shrugs, even though a playful smile stays firmly on his face. "I'm pansexual, sweetheart. Call it whatever you want."

Closing my eyes, a comfortable silence fits over all three of us as the exhaustion well and truly begins to creep up. So, of course, I have to break it and ask questions. "Hey, Sean?"

"Yes, beautiful?"

"Why do we always have sex in the middle of the night?"

Noah snorts into my shoulder, wrapping a possessive arm around my waist. My eyes don't have to be open to know that Sean more than likely is rolling his eyes. He responds to my question with a question of his own. "Why do you always tempt me in the middle of the night? I'm the old man here. I have a bed time, ya know."

That makes Noah pick his head up. "Okay, no. Daddy kink, sure. No old man shit. Hard no."

"I'm turning fifty soon, dumbass."

I can't help the smile that covers my entire face at Sean's response. "And we're turning thirty soon. I probably need a chiropractor as much as you do."

A harsh sequel leaves my mouth when Sean twists one of my nipples over his T-shirt, and my eyes pop wide open. I turn to him, aghast. "What was that for?"

"Because I can now."

I squint at him.

"And you're a brat. And I wanted to see those pretty brown eyes."

"Didn't have enough of them when you were choking me and demanding eye contact?" I retort back.

His answer is firm. "Never."

I turn towards Noah. "How have you dealt with this man for ten years?"

Noah's face turns downright devious. He leans down to whisper in my ear, "With his cock down my throat and filling my ass. He has lots of perks to him."

I take a deep breath.

Okay, yeah. That's really fucking hot.

But it only brings more fucking questions to my mind. Or rather, a statement. "We're going to have to talk about everything, ya know."

Noah nods. Sean smiles.

It's mutually understood though.

Not tonight.

Tonight, we just enjoy what the possibility of an us could even be.

And I'd be lying if I said I didn't feel excited at the prospect.

THE SOUND OF A BUZZING NOISE STIRS ME from sleep. I groan, a pout heavy on my face. When did I even set an alarm? Why does it feel like it's *on* me?

The sound of Noah moaning springs my eyes wide open, just as a deep, masculine chuckle leaves him.

I blink down at myself, disoriented, and gasp.

The fucking buzzing is a vibrator on my clit.

Holy shit.

Turning my head, I find them with their legs scissoring each other, while Sean's fist wraps around both of their lengths, jerking them off simultaneously. The sight of both of their cocks in one hand makes my mouth go downright dry, and a whimper tears out of me as the vibration on my clit turns from an unfamiliar one to one of pleasure.

Both of their eyes stay on me as Sean slowly brings

them both toward climax. He smirks, his voice rough with sleep. "Good morning, beautiful."

My mouth parts.

This shouldn't be so hot, but it really fucking is.

Noah moans as Sean starts flicking his wrist with every upward motion. He tosses his head back, panting, while bearing the majority of his weight on his hands. Their cocks slide together, wet with spit. Then he turns his lustful gaze back on me immediately. "Daddy wanted to play. Can't leave our girl out, though. You wanna play?"

Sean speeds up his stroking at being called Daddy, and both of us cry out—Noah at the feeling of it, and me at the visual of the live-action porno.

My words come out as a whimper. "Is this really happening right now?"

Noah raises a playful eyebrow as he breaths deeply. "Why? Our pretty girl think she's dreaming?"

I nod my head, breathless.

Sitting up as much as he can, Noah pushes firmly on the vibrator that's positioned over my my pussy, allowing him to work us both. My legs spread instantly, hips lifting uncontrollably into the buzzing sensation. My own head falls back down with a moan. Noah grunts. "Not a dream, baby girl. You want to keep using this one or do you need more?"

As sore as I am, I have no hesitation when I beg, "More. Please, more."

Sean growls, turning to me. His fist moves even faster and he nearly bears his teeth from the pleasure coursing through him. "Ya know, I wanted to frot his cock inside of you again. But Noah said no."

I whine. "Now?"

I don't think I could take that much more, so soon.

Even though the idea is a little appealing.

Sean laughs. "No. Not yet. He's right. You need a marginal break. And I love spoiling you, but I can't forget to spoil him too—if we're turning this dynamic into the three of us."

Noah grunts. "I'm good with favoring her."

He turns his gaze back to him, daring Noah to test him. "Oh, I know, *Son*. Me too. But you're still going to take your Daddy's cock. I haven't fucked your ass in way too long." His eyes go back to mine. "And frankly, I own you both now. I'll do whatever the fuck I want."

With Noah's hand still pushing the vibrator into my clit, my legs start to shake at the image of them before me and the words coming from his mouth. "You own me? Us?"

Noah's breathing turns ragged. "We both do. All of us. To each other."

My mouth drops open, my orgasm cresting. Part of me knows I'm coming because of those words, more than anything. And that thought alone is beyond terrifying.

Right when my pussy begins to tingle, me directly on the edge, both men before me fucking *laugh* and pull the vibrator away entirely. I whine. "What? No. Why? I was right there."

Sean's gaze is hard and heavy. "You lied yesterday, little girl. When you told Noah that you didn't know me. Your rules. You lie, you get punished. Consider this a gift—because I know ways to make you cry."

Noah groans. His eyes go back and forth between me and Sean. "Sean, I'm gonna come. Fuck. You want me to come like this?"

Sean leans up, taking his weight off of his other hand, and smacks the tip of Noah's dick. "That's not my fucking name."

He cries out. "Daddy! Fuck!"

With renewed effort, Sean jerks the both of them off like his life depends on it. "Come little one. Come for Daddy. Come right on Daddy's cock. But then you're going to fuck our girlfriend and breed her sweet pussy while I take your ass."

Noah grunts loudly, losing his control. The hand that was previously holding the vibrator to my pussy grips my thigh in a bruising hold, and I watch as

Noah's dick twitches and spills hot cum all over Sean's cock. He's a mess of moans, grunts, and cries. The cum acts as lube between them, adding to Sean's strokes, and Sean and I watch in a complete trance.

Before I can say anything at all, Sean groans loudly. "Fuuuuuck."

Before I know it both of them are coming on each other, sticky cum mixing with sticky cum. It pools around their lengths, coating every single inch of them.

Jesus Christ.

All of that cum was inside of me last night.

And god help me—because I want it every single day for the rest of my life.

They both twitch and shake, sensitive as their orgasms fade. Sean's hand stays around the base of their cocks, holding them firmly together.

I whimper, "I want this every day for the rest of my fucking life."

I watch as both men look at each other and smile from my words. But it's Noah who backs up from Sean, his dick still covered in a mixture of their cum— only to crawl overtop of me. He lifts Sean's T-shirt, exposing my breasts to the cold air, and leans down to suck one into his mouth. Sean rolls over to do the exact same thing, biting into one of my nipples softly. I gasp as both of them suck on me.

After a couple minutes of them licking, sucking,

and biting my flesh, Sean raises his head to kiss me sweetly.

"Ours."

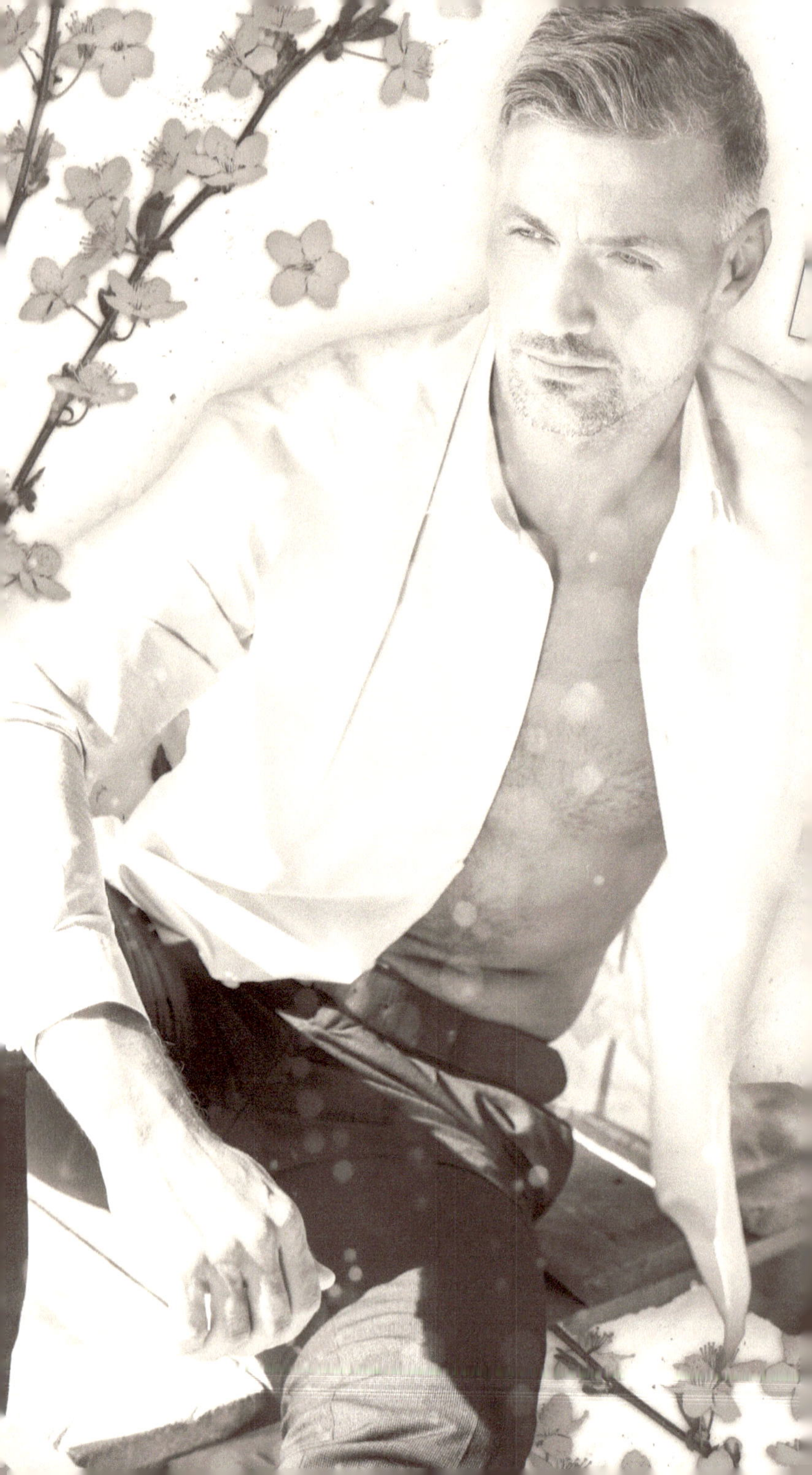

THIRTEEN

SITTING UP, my hand makes its way to my cock, stroking it hard again. Lauren lays beneath the both of us, breathing erratically. Her eyes bounce between Noah and I, the deep browns turning into honey as the morning sunlight from the curtains hits them. With my other hand, I play with a strand of the black parts of her hair. "You're so gorgeous."

She blushes at the compliment, shy.

Fucking adorable.

I want to make them both delirious in this moment.

Losing the last bit of patience I have, I turn away from them both and settle behind Noah. My hands squeeze and grip his asscheeks, spreading him apart.

Without a second thought, I spit on his hole and use a pointer finger to spread it around.

My voice is dark. "Has anyone else been back here since me?"

Noah's voice is shy. "You're the only one who's ever had me there."

Reaching underneath him, I stroke his cock once, covering my hand with some of the cum that still covers him. He shivers at my touch, and I smirk. "Good. I'm the only one who gets to take this ass." I pause, looking at Lauren. "Unless...someone wants to strap one day."

Both of her eyebrows fly up. "Jesus H. Christ."

It makes both of us laugh, only for Noah's to turn into a deep moan when I take my hand off of him and use my cum-covered fingers to thrust into his ass. His hole shapes around me perfectly, almost like no time has passed between us playing at all.

Granted, it's only been six months or so, but still.

I shrug my shoulders. "What? We're gonna have to learn every single thing you like. This isn't just a threesome, little girl. We have a lot to test."

Noah cuts in, "Daddy...Please. Fuck me."

As if it wasn't hard enough, my dick transforms into a steel pole.

Inserting a third finger, I decide he's ready for me. I

pull him back slightly. "Fuck our girlfriend. Go on. Stick it in."

Lauren looks up at me in shock. "You...you meant that? All of us at the same time?"

She hardly gets to finish her sentence before Noah is bottoming out inside her, forcing her head back into the pillows. A raw moan tears itself out of her throat.

I smirk down at her as I push Noah's hips down slightly, probably forcing him right into her damn cervix, and climb the back of his thighs. "I mean everything I say, little girl."

Neither of them get a chance to respond. With Noah's ass still spread, I thrust into him, hissing at the warmth and tightness that immediately chokes my cock. He cries out, gripping Lauren's arm for support.

I pull back, leaving just my tip inside of him. "Yeah, baby?"

He babbles incoherently. "Yes, *yes*, fuck my ass, Daddy. Fuck it."

I thrust right back in, forcing a moan from Lauren. My tone is downright evil. "You wanna know what's different about this time, Noah?"

"Uh-huh?"

I pull out slightly, sliding down his thighs a bit. With my dick half-way seated inside him, I move my hands from his ass to his waist, rocking him back and forth between Lauren and I. The action forces him to fuck Lauren while I fuck him. My words come out harsh, knowing it'll send him into a frenzy. "You're just a Fleshlight for us both, Son."

The change of position and my words make him brainless.

I look at Lauren and point to the vibrator still next to her. "Use that, sweetheart. I know you're sore. And we won't last long."

She doesn't hesitate. She reaches for the toy, turns it on, and shoves it between her and Noah. Coincidently, the vibrator brushes some of Noah's dick, making him shout. "Fuck!"

Growling, I repeat the motions over and over again. Biceps flexing, fingers straining, I repeatedly bounce Noah on my cock, forcing him in and out of Lauren's cunt. The bed squeaks from the weight and force of all of us, and I thank God that my house is big enough to not warrant us a noise complaint, because this is a morning it absolutely could.

Huffing, I focus my attention on Lauren. "You might be a praise-slut, baby girl, but he's the opposite. Just a little whore with a hole that Daddy needs to abuse."

Noah repeats my words, delirious, "Daddy's whore. Just Daddy's whore."

Him affirming it makes me even closer to busting in him.

I groan. "Daddy's whore and Daddy's beautiful little girl, all getting fucked. All taking cock like they were made for it."

Lauren's teeth click together. "I...I can't...I need to..."

Her admission pushes Noah over the edge he was clinging to. He shouts as his orgasm crashes through him without warning. And like dominos, both Lauren and I follow. I continue bouncing Noah through my orgasm, ensuring Lauren is getting fucked through hers, too. It milks every last drop of cum out of my balls, and watching Lauren's eyes roll into the back of her head is more than worth it. Her back arches, tits arching into Noah's face, and he latches onto one, only heightening the sensations for her.

Unable to continue, I release Noah. My chest heaves from the exertion of what we just did, and if I didn't feel so relaxed, I'd think I just completed a workout from hell.

Breathing deep, I pull out of Noah, watching as my load immediately drips out of him.

God, if that's not a sight I missed.

Once I'm out, Noah does the same, pulling out of Lauren. We collapse on either side of her, each throwing an arm over her.

Securing her.

And it feels *right*.

FOURTEEN

LAUREN SITS at the kitchen island, back in her outfit from yesterday, scrolling on her phone. Her hair is tied up in a messy ponytail, her legs crossed delicately underneath the island. I can't keep my hands off of her. Sean stands in front of the stove, already showered, flipping grilled cheeses and whistling under his breath.

How this already feels so normal nearly scares me.

It's never felt this normal. This...happy.

And it's only been one fucking day. Even though we each have history with Lauren, it's only been a day of all three of us.

Coming up behind Lauren, I rest my chin on her shoulder and look at her phone. She's texting a group chat labeled, *Hooligans,* which forces a chuckle out of me.

Reading it with her, my chuckle grows into full-on laughter.

LAUREN

> How do you guys do this threesome thing every day?
>
> Not like, romantically. That's fine. Sexually, I mean.

CASEY

Come again????

RORY

Uhm...sis, what.

LAUREN

Answers first, questions last.

RORY

Lube, stretches, and proper aftercare to make you want to continue.

CASEY

Lauren you can't be asking me that

LAUREN

Why not?? You deal with Aiden. So you have to deal with me too.

RORY

She has a point, love.

CASEY

Yeah but now I'm thinking of Aiden's sister's sex life! That's not cool!!!

LAUREN

Pussy.

CASEY

attached gif of Suicide Squad, "I will knock yo ass out."

RORY

Alright, messaging you privately. I need the tea. The baby is pouting now.

(Casey. Not the actual baby.)

CASEY

HEY!

I shake my head, utterly amused with the conversation. Sean turns around, plating the grilled cheeses and looking at us suspiciously. "What?"

I rat her out immediately. "She's asking her brother- and sister-in-law about their threesomes and how to survive us."

Sean's mouth drops. "Is your brother in that chat?"

Lauren almost drops her phone. "Ew, no!"

I chortle. "For now. Aiden's husband might add him just to save himself."

"Pfft," Lauren scoffs. "He'd never. He's a golden retriever to his core."

Taking my plate of grilled cheese, I move to sit on Lauren's left while Sean sits on her right. "You told me you had another brother. You don't talk about him much. Why?"

Immediately, Lauren sets down her phone, even as Rory's name starts repeatedly flashing. She stares at the counter contemplating. "Yeah, Cole. He, uh...he kinda distanced himself from Aiden and I when our father died. I can't blame him, though. He's the youngest and literally all of his core memories are abuse *or* us being abused. He told us that he'll be coming home in a year or so, I think. But I don't know."

Sean nods his head. "Where's he at?"

"California's his home, but he's somewhere in the Middle East, currently."

Sean's brows scrunch together in confusion. I roll my eyes. "Hey, *stepdaddy*, you know we're both military, right? Why else would he live somewhere with a base, but be in the Middle East?"

Understanding dawns...then he turns to me with that fucking *dad* look he gets when I have a smart mouth. I bite into my grilled cheese to hide my smirk.

Lauren continues. "Yeah. I miss him. Just hope he

comes home safe. He's absolutely the most reckless out of all of us."

That piques my interest. "What do you mean?"

She worries the top of her lip. "You know those TikTok accounts that are full of masked men and stuff? Yeah. I found his. But it's darker than just thirst traps. It just worries me."

Sean's eyebrows fly up. "Alright, I'd join TikTok for that, actually."

Lauren slaps his shoulder which forces a choked laugh out of me. "Careful now. You can't have me *and* my brother."

Sean leans down to whisper in her ear, even though I can clearly hear. "I meant the thirst traps, jealous girl. My hands are going to be quite full with just you and this one over here." His head juts towards me.

I break the ice with the question that I know has been plaguing all of us. "So, this is it, right? We're a unit?"

Silence surrounds us for a second. Then Sean speaks first. "I want to be."

"I do, too."

Our gaze falls on Lauren. She looks at both of us, confused. "Why would I let both of you fuck my vagina at the same goddamn time if I didn't want this? I'll probably never be the same. It's a miracle I don't need a wheelchair right now."

My mouth drops at that answer.

I thought she would have gone lovey-dovey. Not say *that*.

Sean pauses. "Even if that means you belong solely to us? Dealing with us in all ways of the definition?"

I admit my one worry before she can answer. "Even though he was my stepdad?"

She sets down her grilled cheese and looks at me patiently. "As far as anyone else knows, we're just a throuple who scored a hot sugar daddy. No one knows your past, and no one has to. You're not gross. Either of you." She turns to look at Sean. "And I told you the very first day I met you that I've spent my entire life feeling lonely and clueless as to where I belong, and how your dynamic sounded nice. Being fully owned by two. Never lonely. Never longing. Just...happy. Of course, I want that."

Emotions claw their way up my throat to the point that I fear my voice will crack if I try to speak. Sean watches her intently as she continues. "You two had some women who didn't know what they wanted, or who just wanted threesomes. It sucks, and I'm sorry that jaded you, but I'm not them. I'm telling you I want you both in every single way. And I mean it. Will I need to learn some things, sure. But when don't you learn things in a new relationship?"

Sean and I look at each other at the exact same

time, tears in our eyes. All insecurities, well and truly vanish.

Sean was right when he talked about that one-night stand.

She is truly the one.

Want to see more from the characters in the Reckless Hearts world? Well... they may or may not have cameos coming ;)

Click here to pre-order Book Three in the Reckless Hearts Series.

Continue on to read the Epilogue of Clueless <3

8 MONTHS LATER

HOOLIGANS
CASEY

If I add Aiden or Cole to this group
chat, will he see prior texts?

RORY

No baby.

CASEY

Omg thank you

I've been scared about that for days

RORY

You know you could have just
started another group chat, right?

ME

That may have been too advanced
for Casey

CASEY

Lauren, I swear to God, I won't lift a
single one of your OR Noah's boxes
if you keep bullying me.

ME

I SEND the text with tears rolling down my face, laughing harder than I have all day. Sean and Noah peek their head at me from the suite bathroom, nosy as always.

RORY

Hey, why ARE we lifting so much?
Isn't Sean, like, bookoo rich?

CASEY

YEAH!

ME

You guys know you're not lifting
anything, right?

Noah and I have been moved in for
a full week now. We just finished
unpacking last night.

It's just a party.

CASEY

head explosion gif

*CASEY HAS ADDED AIDEY-POO AND
COLE •• TO THE CHAT*
CASEY

We've been miscommunicated to.

AIDEN

Why am I in here? I'm literally laying
next to the both of you.

AIDEY-POO HAS LEFT THE CHAT

ME

Rude.

I turn toward the men still staring at me from the bathroom doorway. "Sibling chat."

That's all they need to hear before nodding and going back to doing whatever the hell boys do to get ready.

COLE

What timc?

I swallow roughly and blink at the short and curt response from my second brother. It's normal for Aiden to be an ass, but what's not normal is for Cole to respond at all.

Progress, I guess.

ME

3 p.m.

COLE

I sigh, tossing my phone down. At least he responded this time.

As punctual as ever, Cole is the first person to arrive—three o'clock on the dot. I watch as he gets out of the passenger seat of the car, crutches and leg brace keeping him stable. "Do you need help?" I call out.

His blond hair, so pale it may as well reflect the sunlight, shifts in the wind as he shakes his head. It's the only trait he got from our mother. The rest of him is completely Dad.

I swallow.

I don't need to psychoanalyze him to know that fucks with him more than anything.

Walking to him anyway, I grab the backpack from the asphalt. I raise a brow in question. It's unlike him to bring an entire backpack somewhere.

His voice is gruff. "Stuff to do if it gets too loud."

My heart pangs.

I've seen him a few times since the accident.

Not enough.

I don't press it, or him, though.

I wave to the Uber driver—a young woman who looks more in love with my brother than a school girl with her first crush—and start trekking back up to Sean's house.

My house.

Our house.

That'll never not be weird as fuck.

As soon as the Uber driver pulls out of the driveway, Aiden's truck pulls into its place. It brings a laugh out of my chest as I stare at my driveway, full of trucks and military men and or military wives. It probably says way too much about me to have that type—but it extending to my brothers is a whole different story.

Opening the door for everyone, they file in in a single line behind Cole who aims straight for the food. Seraphina—Rory, Aiden, and Casey's daughter— walks ever so slowly as she's still learning to walk, with a very pregnant Rory walking equally as slow. Aiden and Casey watch them both, utterly captivated, and my heart swells.

It swells until I look back at Cole, who looks utterly crushed, watching everyone enter.

Catching me watching him, he coughs and turns back to the food.

Aiden and Casey give me sideways hugs while Rory nearly tackles me, just as Sean and Noah step into the house from the garage.

They waste no time reminding everyone why they're here.

My eyes roll as I shut the door. *Fucking military men.* There has to be a point right away or no point at all.

Sean coughs awkwardly. "So, you're all obviously here for a reason."

Casey pouts. "Yeah, I thought we were moving you two in. What the fuck?"

Aiden pats Casey's head, making him pout more as the rest of us laugh. Sean continues. "First, I just want to thank all of you for allowing me into your lives an—"

I cut him off, holding up my left hand and rescuing every single person from the cringey *dad* speech they were all about to get. "WE'RE GETTING MARRIED!"

Aiden's mouth drops open.

Casey and Rory smile big and bright.

Cole blinks a few times before the ghost of a smile crosses his face, too.

And as Noah raises his hand, showing off his band, too, Sean only shakes his head and laughs. Because he's absolutely used to our dynamic by now, and he wouldn't have it any other way.

I walk to him anyway and kiss him sweetly before turning to Noah to do the same.

Our lives started way before the rings.

But a girl has to be extra and show it off anyway.

WANT MORE FROM C. S. SILVERNE?

SOLO RELEASES

Preyless: An MMF Military Romance

Clueless: An MMF Forbidden Romance

Faceless: An MM Military Romance

Longing for More: A Forbidden Military MFM

Contrition: A Second Chance MFM Rockstar

Prideful Ache: An Age Gap Romance

CO-WRITES WITH TILLY RIDGE:

Play The Game: A Dark Masked Why Choose Romance

Ride the Line: An MMF Forbidden Romance

Run the Night: An FFM Age Gap Romance

Birdie: A Small Town Sapphic Romance

Guardbait: An MMM Dark Romance

ACKNOWLEDGMENTS

To everyone in my life who has given me courage to keep living, despite going through some really tough stuff once upon a time. This list is pretty endless and I wouldn't know where to start with names if I tried. Honestly, I'm sure there are complete strangers I've only spoken to once that would fit this bill. But...I wouldn't be here without them. Genuinely. Thank you.

To Sadie, who rescued me when I needed it and was doubting my path. I can't thank you enough for everything you've done. I'm so thankful to be in your roster now.

To Tilly, who had to listen to me bitch about this storyline for quite a while—which is hilarious given her feelings about the military and... well, men in general. That's how you know you've hit "Oh, we're good friends" level, huh?

To Bria, who continues to help me grow every day, and without her, I'd be a flailing fish in the sea. Seriously. I don't know how she does it. I'm tired for her.

And lastly, to T—my best friend and bestest supporter. I wouldn't be here without you. There's so much that I could say here... but honestly, I'll just cry, and we both know that I do enough of that as-is. Just, thank you. My yellow heart, always. <3

ABOUT C. S. SILVERNE

C. S. Silverne is a twenty-something year old author who spends a lot of her time hiding behind a computer as the true introvert she is—between writing words, designing pretty pictures, reading her kindle, or blaring the latest rock/country music release—it's guaranteed she's trying to ignore the world in some fashion.

Even in her dark/forbidden and occasionally taboo writing styles... she takes light of her pseudonym, always finding love in the silver linings of the world. Because, as we all know, sometimes—love chooses us in the strangest, cruelest of ways, and the stories of the forbidden deserved to be told.

Find C. S. Silverne here:
https://www.cssilverneauthor.com/